Sunny Hills

Issaquah School District #411
SUNNY HILLS ELEMENTARY
565 N. W. Holly St.
Issaquah, WA 98027

GIT ALONG, OLD SCUDDER

by Stephen Gammell

LOTHROP, LEE & SHEPARD BOOKS/NEW YORK

To Jay and Jon

Library of Congress Cataloging in Publication Data
Gammell, Stephen.
Git along, Old Scudder.
Summary: Old Scudder doesn't know where he is
until he draws a map and names the places on it.
[1. West (U.S.)—Fiction.   2. Maps—Fiction]   I. Title.
PZ7.G144Gi   1983   [E]   82-13996
ISBN 0-688-01674-X   ISBN 0-688-01677-4 (lib. bdg.)

Back in the early 1800s, names like Jim Bridger, Old Bill Williams, Broken Hand Fitzpatrick, and Joe Meek were well known. These mountain men spent their time in the western United States, trapping, hunting, and exploring.

Some of these fellows, like Old Scudder, weren't well known at all. But you can still see places they found today, if you know where to look.

Here's Old Scudder to tell about it himself…

HOW-DO, childrun. Once Old Scudder stayed out in the
wilderness so long, I got a mite confused. Not lost, mind ye.
Jes' seeing to m' traps and looking fer beaver.
This ol' varmint never was lost.

But you kin get t' feeling spookity, alone in the mountains,
and one day I plumb didn't know whar I was at.
So I drew m'self a map.

"Bear grits! Now I know whar Old Scud is! And thar's the fort yonder! I'll gather m' stuff and head on over that way."

So I did.

Hop-skipping down the mountain,

carefully studying m' map,

this ol' possum arrived

at the fort.

But I never did care much 'bout sitting still.
After a little rest, me and m' new friend thought
to travel on some.

"Pilgrim," says I, "got me a notion to put more on this map than a fort 'n' a mountain. Reckon thar's plenty to see hereabouts. What say you and I git along?"

Wahl now, that's what we did. Took the road from the fort.

SNEAKY TREE ROAD, I reckoned.
Got to put it on m' map. Yessir!

Across the plains we went, past an ornery-looking rock.
RED BULL BUTTE, I calls it. Wouldn't you?

Happened to look back after a time.
That's TWO NOSE PASS we come through,
sure as m' moccasins smell.

But there's something Old Scudder cain't figure.

Maybe you'll know...

WHAR ARE WE, ANYHOW?

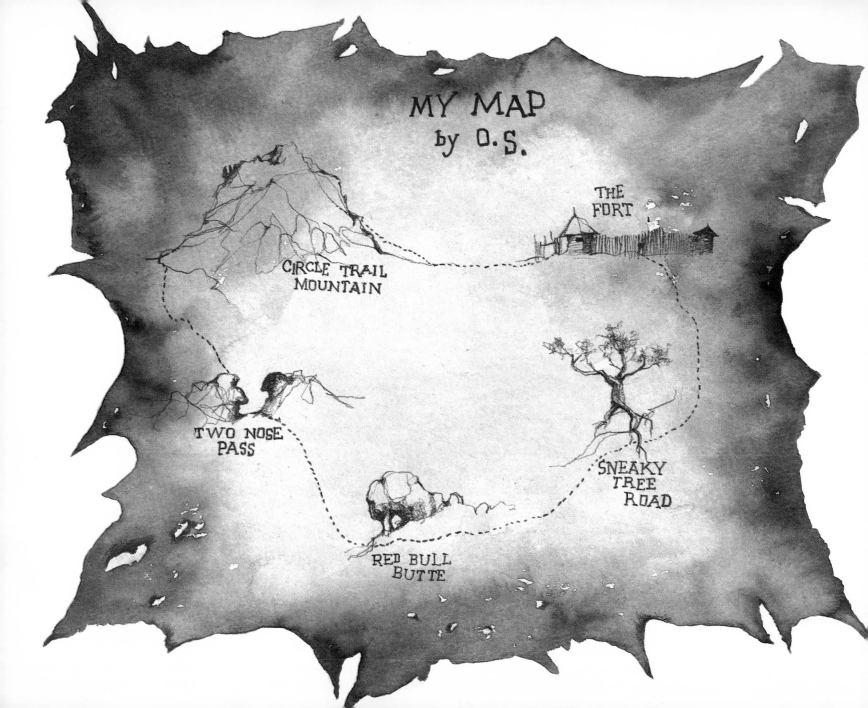